Hosni the Dreamer

AN ARABIAN TALE

Ehud Ben-Ezer

Pictures by URI SHULEVITZ

FARRAR STRAUS GIROUX

NEW YORK

Text copyright © 1997 by Ehud Ben-Ezer. Illustrations copyright © 1997 by
Uri Shulevitz. All rights reserved. Published simultaneously in Canada by
HarperCollins *CanadaLtd.* Color separations by Hong Kong Scanner Arts. Printed
and bound in the United States of America by Berryville Graphics. Designed by
Marjorie Zaum. First edition, 1997

Library of Congress Cataloging-in-Publication Data
Ben-'Ezer, Ehud, date.
   Hosni the dreamer : an Arabian tale / Ehud Ben-'Ezer; pictures by Uri
Shulevitz. — 1st ed.
     p.   cm.
   Summary: Hosni, a shepherd living in the desert, finally realizes his
dream of traveling to the city where he spends his gold dinar in a way
which changes his life forever.
    [1. Shepherds—Fiction. 2. Deserts—Fiction. 3. Dreams—Fiction.] I.
Shulevitz, Uri, date. ill. II. Title.
PZ7.B4245Ho 1997
[E]—DC20   96-18608

Hosni was a shepherd who worked for a sheikh. He was
alone during the day, and since he had no one to talk to, he
would sometimes talk to his sheep.

After work, the shepherds liked to spend their evenings
joking with one another, or discussing what they would buy if
they had money. All but Hosni.

He preferred to spend his evenings listening to the tribal
elders' tales of travel and adventure in faraway cities. Hosni had
always lived in the desert, and their stories filled him with
dreams.

One night, Hosni dreamed that he was in a city. The dream seemed so real to him that he felt he had actually been there. He wanted to tell the other shepherds about it, but he was afraid they would laugh at him.

Instead, he told his dream to his sheep.

One of the shepherds overheard him and said to the others,
"Hosni talks nonsense to his sheep!"

"How strange," said one.

"How stupid," said another. Soon all the shepherds were
making fun of him.

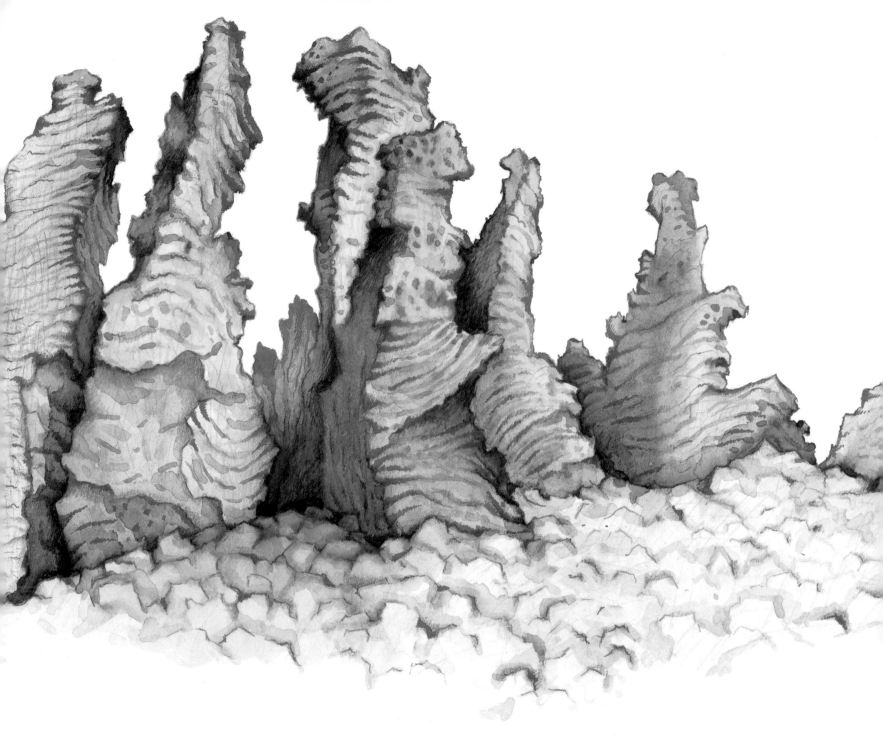

One day, the sheikh wanted to sell some of his camels in the city. He decided to take several of his shepherds on this journey, but Hosni wasn't one of them.

When Hosni begged the sheikh to let him go, the sheikh said, "Sorry, Hosni. Maybe next time."

Then, just when they were ready to leave, one of the shepherds fell ill. The sheikh decided to let Hosni take the sick man's place.

They traveled for days, going through canyons, passing over mountains. Hosni felt so lucky to be going to the city that he didn't even notice how hot and dry it was.

After crossing a large wadi—a riverbed that was dry—they finally reached the city.

The sheikh sold his camels. He paid each shepherd a gold dinar and gave them the rest of the day off to enjoy the wonders of the city.

The shepherds hurried off together, leaving Hosni on his own.

Hosni wandered through the city's streets, amid the noisy
crowd. The more he walked, the more the city felt like his
dream, and like the tribal elders' tales. Only now it was real, and
even more exciting than he had imagined.

He went to the city's market, passing by the shops and
stands with their colorful cloth, embroidered robes, carpets,
shiny pots and plates. The scent of pilaf, kebab, falafel, couscous,
and sweet halvah filled the air. But Hosni didn't buy anything.

Then he noticed a sign on a small shop: "One verse for one gold dinar."

Hosni felt he must go in.

When he entered, he found himself in a different world, where he could no longer hear the noise and commotion of the market.

An old man was sitting alone.

Hosni gave the old man his gold dinar. The man took the
coin, studied Hosni carefully, then slowly pronounced, "Don't
cross the water until you know its depth." Hosni waited. Finally,
he asked, "Is that all, sir?"

The old man said no more.

The next morning, Hosni, the sheikh, and the shepherds left the city and rode into the desert.

On the way, the shepherds talked about all they had eaten and all they had bought in the city. They asked Hosni what he bought. Hosni didn't respond. Then they began teasing him for not purchasing anything and for wasting his trip to the city.

Finally, Hosni blurted out, "I did buy something. A verse!"

"A verse?" They could hardly believe their ears. He told
them the verse, and they burst out laughing. "He spends all his
money on worthless nonsense," said one.

"What a foolish fool," said yet another, laughing. And the
sheikh laughed, too.

The shepherds were still laughing when they noticed dark
rain clouds in the distance. They knew from the lightning and
thunder that there must be a violent downpour in the mountains
above them. But the rain was far away, and not a single drop fell
on them.

They soon came to the wadi that had been dry on their way
to the city, and now rainwater from the mountains was flowing
in it.

The sheikh and the shepherds didn't hesitate. They entered
the water with their loaded-down camels and began crossing.

Hosni thought about the verse he had bought, and stopped.
"Don't cross the water until you know its depth," he repeated to
himself. Hosni called to the sheikh and the shepherds to come
back. But the sheikh replied impatiently, "Hurry up, Hosni!"

Now, a richly dressed man was also standing by the wadi.
He was leading a camel by a long rope. On top of the camel was
a luxurious canopy.

When the man saw the sheikh and the shepherds begin to cross the wadi, he, too, entered the water. Hosni tried to warn him, but the man just shrugged his shoulders and kept going.

Though Hosni did not want to be left behind, he kept thinking about the verse and couldn't bring himself to cross.

The others hadn't gone far when suddenly

a swift and powerful undercurrent swept them away and the
rushing water swallowed them up.

Hosni was horrified by what had happened.

Then he heard a voice from inside the canopy on the
camel's back. "My poor, poor servant! Oh, how awful!"

Hosni approached the canopy and discovered a young
maiden in it.

"Gracious sir," she said. "I'm Zobeide. Now that my servant has perished, I'm lost. Please, help me."

"Don't worry," Hosni said gently. "I can take you back to the city."

"Oh, no! Not there," she said. "I don't want to return to the Emir. Against my wishes, he has sent me as a present to a prince I don't know. Where are you heading?"

"I have no family," said Hosni. "Now that the sheikh is dead, I have no work either. Besides, I'd rather go to an entirely new place than return to one where I was unhappy."

"Please, let me travel with you," said Zobeide.

Hosni tied the rope of Zobeide's camel to his. He didn't attempt to cross the rushing waters. Instead, he went around the entire length of the wadi.

They traveled for a long time. The days were very hot and the nights were cold.

Hosni told Zobeide what he had learned from the tribal elders, of his dream about a city he had never seen before, and how the old man sold him a verse that saved him from the terrible tragedy they had witnessed.

Zobeide told Hosni, "My father had worked for the Emir. After I became an orphan, I was raised in the Emir's palace. Life there wasn't as happy as you would think. Although I am most disturbed by what happened at the wadi, I believe it was a sign that I wasn't meant to live in another palace with an unknown prince."

Finally, they came to another city.
Hosni and Zobeide grew to love each other.

Soon they were married. With the silver and gold that
Zobeide's camel carried, they bought a large house and fields.

In time, they raised a family, and lived happily for many
years. Hosni never forgot the old man and his verse.